Yah's Wild Gift of Imagination

written by
Gene G. Bradbury

illustrated by
Roxanne Grinstad

**BookWilde
Children's Books**

Yah's Wild Gift of Imagination

Book prepress: Kate Weisel, weiselcreative.com

All inquiries should be addressed to

BookWilde Children's Books
422 Williamson Rd.
Sequim, WA 98382

or visit our website
genegbradbury.com

**BookWilde
Children's Books**

Author's Dedication

To all those who enjoy stories and the surprises they bring to our lives.
And to the child in us all who continues to delight in mystery and imagination.

— Gene G. Bradbury

Illustrator's Dedication

To our creator God who gifted us with our planet Earth!
And to my loving husband Dick, children Ian and Gigi, my brother Ken and parents
Howard and Jean who from the very beginning blessed my desire to paint.

— Roxanne Celeste Grinstad

In the very very beginning,
darkness filled the universe.

Not even a night-light
shone in space.

Yah moved over the darkness
and said,

"It is so empty! There is no light or land or sea or sky. I see no planets, sun, moon, or stars."

"Where are the swimming things?
Where are the wild things?

Where are the creepy-crawly things?
Where are the flying-whirly things?"

"There is no light or land or sea or sky,
but what if . . .

I see no planets, sun,
moon, or stars,
but what if . . ."

"There are no swimming things
or wild things or creepy-crawly things or
flying-whirly things, but what if . . ."

Yah called upon his wild imagination,
and laughed.

"I HAVE A PERFECTLY WONDERFUL IDEA!"

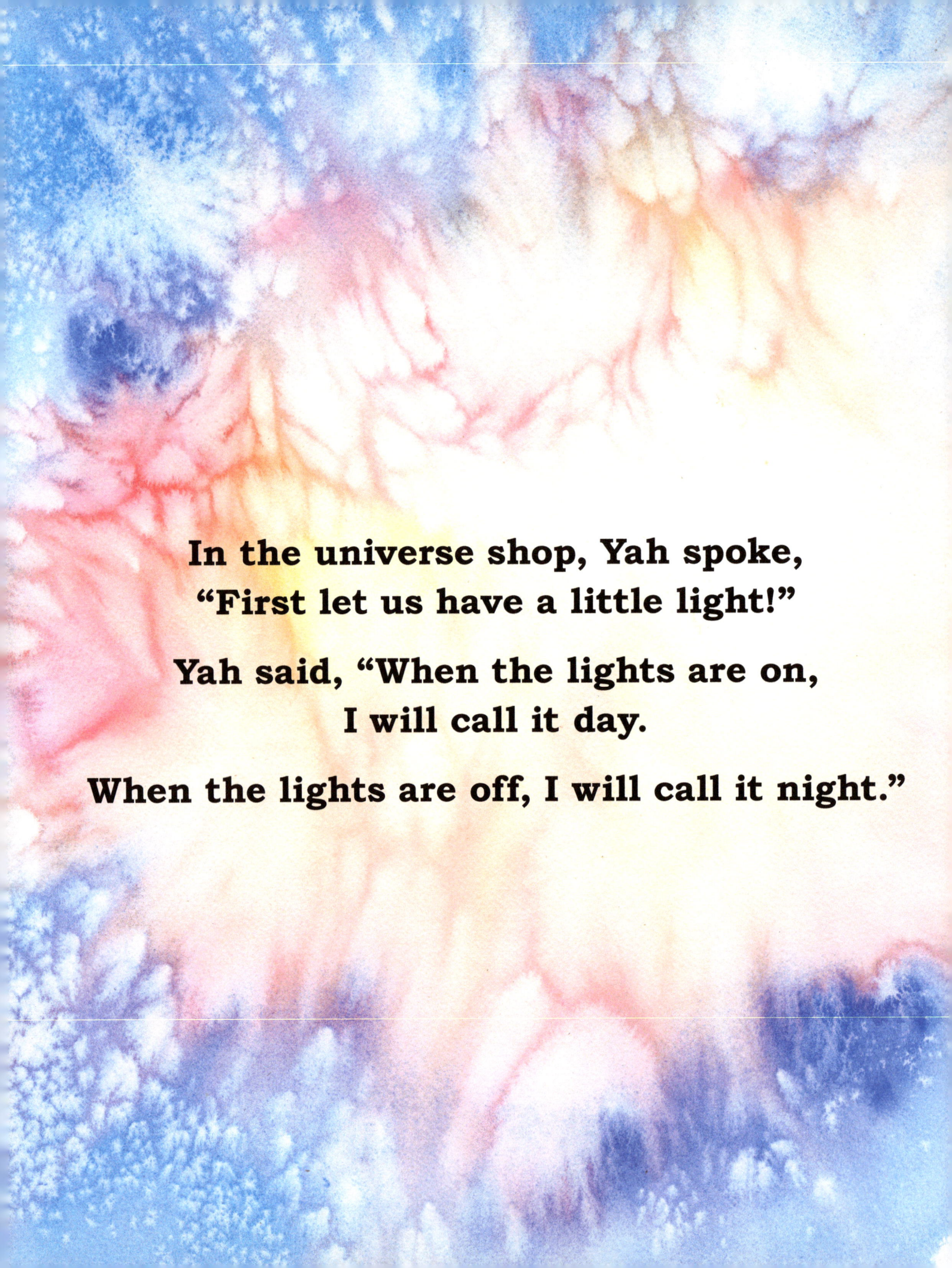

In the universe shop, Yah spoke,
"First let us have a little light!"

Yah said, "When the lights are on,
I will call it day.

When the lights are off, I will call it night."

And Yah said, "THIS IS TOV!"
(Which is a very ancient word that means VERY GOOD!)
"THIS IS TOV!" said Yah. "I LIKE IT!"

Yah worked every day in the universe shop.

The dark and empty world began to fill up.

First the light, then the land, sea, and sky.

Then the planets, sun, moon, and stars.

R.Grinstad

The universe filled with swimming things,

wild things,

creepy-
crawly
things,

and flying-whirly things.

With each new thing Yah made,
Yah said, "THIS IS TOV! I LIKE IT!"

One day Yah said, "I want to make a
school bus and a taxi cab. I want to
make boats and airplanes."

"OH NO!" said Yah.
"Swimming things swim.
Wild things roar.
They don't drive school buses!"

Creepy crawly things creep and crawl; They don't drive taxi cabs !

"Flying-whirly things fly.
They don't fly airplanes!"

THEN YAH HAD A PERFECTLY WONDERFUL IDEA!

"I will make two-legged things
to invent wheels, gears, and wings."

"I will make two-legged things that have a wild imagination like mine."

This is Tov! I like it!

"I will make two-legged things to drive school buses, taxi cabs, and boats. I will make two-legged things to fly airplanes."

TOV SCHOOL

TAXI

As the universe filled up
with wonderful things, Yah spoke,
"There is one more thing I must make."

Yah filled the universe with . . .

PILLOWS! Yah called the pillows
"rest" which means. . .

"Stop working and enjoy the things
Yah has made."

Yah was very pleased with what Yah had made,
and Yah said, "THIS IS TOV! I LIKE IT!"

And all creation
rested . . .

And so should you.

Author's Acknowledgments

On the publication of my twenty-first book, it's time to thank those who have made my publications possible. My wife, Deborah, has faithfully read and edited my work during the ten years of these publications. The person responsible for formatting and providing the technical work of my books is Kathleen Weisel of weiselcreative.com. Kathleen has designed and completed all twenty-one books. This particular book is also the result of diligent work by Roxanne Grinstad who has told the story in beautiful illustrations. Besides these faithful workers are those friends and strangers who have encouraged me in my writing. Last of all are the children who have responded to my books at school visitations with smiles and questions.

Illustrator's Acknowledgments

I am so grateful to our Lord for the magnificent creation we are blessed with!

Heartfelt thanks to my husband Dick, children Ian and Gigi, and our whole family for their encouragement and support.

Each of my painting mentors Esther McLatchy, Bart Rulon, Karlyn Holman, Bonnie Broitzman, Ning and Lingchi Yeh has taught me skills I have used in this book.

Photographer friends Ken and Mary Campbell, Bart Rulon, Audrey Schwartz, Vicky Grady, Judy Bishop and David Sellers shared photo references to help fill my ark with creatures for these pages.

Lifelong friends Dave and Marilyn, Bill and Sue, Gary and Linda hosted and helped me in so many ways!

Adding life to the pages were people who were models for my paintings: Dick, Gigi, Ian, Sandra, Rachel, Julianna, and Annabel.

My gratitude goes to all people working to preserve our Earth and creatures. Especially Arnold and Debbie Schouten, the Olympic Game Farm, and Padilla Bay Reserve. At these places I was able to meet and photograph some delightful animals who appear in this story.

Thank you to Chris Terrell, Keith Eyer and everyone at *How it Works* of Anacortes whose excellence and diligence in archiving my images over the years has made my work possible.

I extend a heartfelt thank you to the family of the late Rachel Braun. Rachel was my dear friend and fellow painter of nature. Her deep love of God and our Earth's creatures continues to be an inspiration to me and all who knew her.

— Roxanne Grinstad

BookWilde Children's Books

Children's Books by the Author

These books are illustrated by watercolorist Victoria Wickell-Stewart.

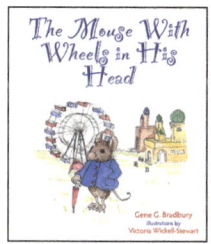

The Mouse With Wheels in His Head. Meet Fergus who wants to be the first mouse to ride the new Ferris Wheel at the World's Fair. Can a tiny mouse find a way to hitch a ride without being discovered? Follow Fergus's adventure at the 1893 Chicago Exhibition.

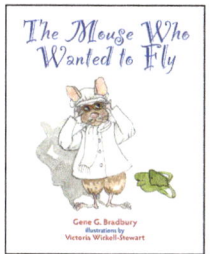

The Mouse Who Wanted to Fly. Adventure is in Fergus's blood. His success in riding the Ferris Wheel is in the past. When Fergus learns that two brothers, Orville and Wilbur, are going to fly the first powered airplane, Fergus is eager for a new adventure. Is it possible that a mouse can be on the first flight at Kitty Hawk?

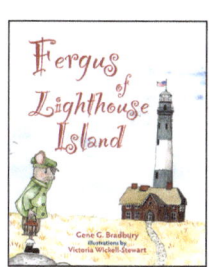

Fergus of Lighthouse Island. Fergus, unlike his great uncle, isn't brave at all. He isn't looking for adventure. But when a hurricane threatens Lighthouse Island, adventure finds him. What will Fergus decide when the hurricane threatens the residents of Mouse Village? It's no place for a mouse who is afraid.

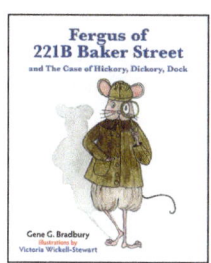

Fergus of 221B Baker Street *and The Case of Hickory, Dickory, Dock:* Haven't you always wanted to know why the mouse ran up the clock? Of course, it's a mystery. Fergus visits his uncle in England, Uncle Delbert lives behind the walls of the very house where Sherlock Holmes the famous detective lives. With his deerstalker hat and Mr. Homes' magnifying glass, Fergus sets out to solve the mystery. But there is one thing Fergus does not count on.

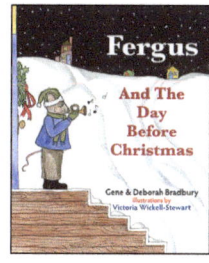

Fergus And The Day Before Christmas. Come and help Fergus and his friends load Santa's sleigh on Christmas Eve. The time is short and the job must be done in one day. Can all the presents be carried from Santa's workshop in time for Christmas?

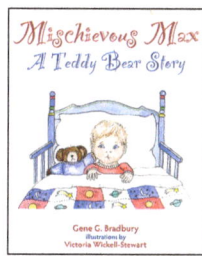

Mischievous Max, A Teddy Bear Story. In Leon's room you will find many teddy bears. Most of them are soft and wonderful to take to bed. But there is one bear who Leon never takes to bed. His name is Max Bear and his fur tickles and his eyes are beastly. Leon knows something else about Max Bear. What if Leon tries sleeping with Max Bear for just one night? Would that be so bad? Leon is about to find out.

The Star Tree. "Do the forest animals know about Christmas?" asks Jody. With her grandfather, Jody goes into the forest to the place where the animals gather on Christmas Eve. Jody discovers that the world is a beautiful place to live. The Star Tree invites children to look for Christmas in the natural world.

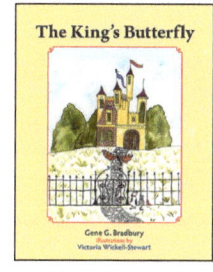

The King's Butterfly invites children to enjoy and respect the beautiful Monarch Butterfly. When the King and Queen capture the butterfly to keep it for a royal pet, they soon find out that a butterfly is meant to fly free. Will they set the butterfly free that it might return again the next year? Perhaps Wizdrop the Wizard has the answer.

◈

These next two books are illustrated by Jean Wyatt.

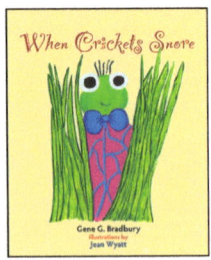

When Crickets Snore is a delightful look at the private life of those singing crickets. It's based on what Henry David Thoreau tells us . . . *In the morning the crickets snore, in the afternoon they chirp, at midnight they dream.* Do they really snore? Page through the lovely illustrations by Jean Wyatt and see for yourself. But read quietly, as the crickets may be in their pajamas.

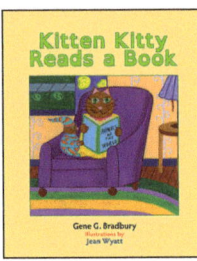

Kitten Kitty Reads a Book invites children to sit on a parent's lap and read a favorite storybook. But what happens when the doorbell rings? When kittens line up outside with their favorite books, will there be room for one kitten more? Beautifully illustrated by Jean Wyatt, children will love to hear the doorbell ring.

Illustrations by artist Roxanne Grinstad.

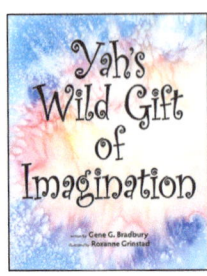

Yah's Wild Gift of Imagination begins in the swirl of darkness. But the light of Yah's wonderful and surprising imagination brings colorful life to the universe. You will marvel at the creepy-crawly things, the flying-whirly things, and the beautiful gifts created in Yah's workshop. Enjoy the wonderful imagination and **illustrations by artist Roxanne Grinstad.**

◈

These books are for 7 to 10 year olds.

Cloud Climber. What were his parents thinking, leaving him for three boring weeks at his grandparent's farm? There would be no internet or cable television and what was worse, only Cousin Emily for company. But on a trip to town with his grandfather, Seth learns of Three Friends Hill and the Banshee's Cave. Are these linked to the discovery of a giant kite Seth and Emily find in the old barn? The three weeks literally fly past and the cousins find that Boring Farm is not so boring after all. **Illustrated by Hannah Bradbury.**

Bedtime Stories To Make You Smile is the first in a series of bedtime books for young children. In this collection of seven stories the intent is to bring a smile to the reader and send them to sleep with happy dreams. Meet William, a bee who doesn't want to be a bee, and Mr. Mouse who loves to read. Aunt Bessie's Elephants may scare you, but just a little. You'll find Boxcar Basset hurtling down the tracks, but not alone. A goldfish tale illustrates that safe driving has benefits for everyone. **Illustrated by Hannah Bradbury.**

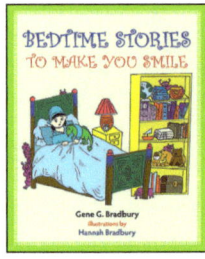

Short Stories Under Four Feet is a gift before bedtime. All the stories in this selection are short enough to read before going to sleep. None of them are over four pages and can slip easily under a pillow or on a dresser or table. Put on your pajamas and find out how a tree becomes the universe and how a dog, called Lion, brings chaos to the kitchen. Perhaps you would rather read about dancing with Orcas or making pretzels. It's all found between these pages.

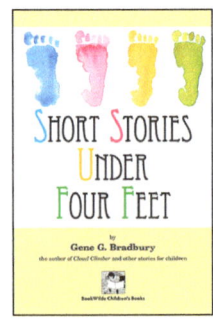

All books available at genegbradbury.com, Amazon.com. barnesandnoble.com, and other retail outlets.